WEEKLY READER
CHILDREN'S BOOK CLUB

WEEKLY READER
CHILDREN'S BOOK CLUB
presents

THE
HORSE
WHO LIVED
UPSTAIRS

BY

PHYLLIS McGINLEY

ILLUSTRATED BY

HELEN STONE

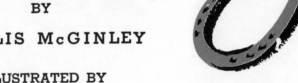

J. B. LIPPINCOTT COMPANY

There was once a horse named Joey

who was discontented.

He was discontented because

he didn't live in

a red barn

with a weathervane

on top

like this,

and he didn't live in a

could run about and kick

green meadow where he

up his heels like this.

Instead, he lived

upstairs
in a big
brick building
in New York.

Joey worked for Mr. Polaski who sold
fruits and vegetables to city people.

Joey pulled the vegetable wagon
through the city streets.

And in New York,

there isn't room
for barns or meadows.

So every night when Joey came home, he stepped out from the shafts of the wagon, and into an elevator, and up he went to his stall on the fourth floor of the big brick building. It was a fine stall and Joey was very comfortable there. He had plenty of oats to eat and plenty of fresh straw to lie on.

He even had a window
to look out of.

But still Joey was discontented.

"How I long to sip fresh water from a babbling brook!" he often exclaimed. And then he would sniff discontentedly at the old bathtub near the elevator which served him as a watering trough.

It wasn't that he had to work hard. Mr. Polaski was kind to him and brought him home at five o'clock every day. In the winter Joey had a blanket to wear on his back to keep him warm.

And in the summer time Mr. Polaski
got him a hat to wear on his head to
keep him cool.

And every day he had many interesting adventures. Sometimes he met
a Policeman who gave him sugar.

Sometimes ladies patted him on

the nose and fed him carrots.

He was introduced to the high-bred horses who drew the hansom cabs along the Plaza.

He saw the children playing in

But it made no difference to Joey.

the playgrounds and the parks.

"This is no life for a horse,"

he used to say to the Percheron who lived in the next stall to him. "We city horses don't know what real living is. I want to move to the country and sleep in a red barn with a weathervane on top, and kick up my heels in a green meadow."

So how happy he was when one day Mr. Polaski said to him, "Joey, I think I could sell more vegetables if I drove a truck. I will miss you, Joey, but you will like it on the farm where I am going to send you."

The next morning a big motor van rolled up. Joey got inside, and away he went to the country. Of course he said goodbye

to the Percheron.
"Goodbye, Joey,"
called his friend.

"I hope
you will be
contented on the farm."

When Joey reached the country, sure enough, there was the barn with its weathervane, and there was the meadow.

"This is the life!" cried Joey to himself.

But poor Joey!

The barn was cold in winter and hot in summer. He didn't have a blanket and he didn't have a hat. And he had very little time to kick up his heels in the green meadow, for all day long he pulled a plow through the earth.

A plow is harder to pull than a wagon, and besides, the farmer worked from sunrise to sundown instead of the eight hours Joey was used to.

Sometimes they forgot to put fresh straw in his stall, and nobody thought to give him sugar or carrots.

There were plenty of children but they climbed on his back and teased him when he wanted to eat. And instead of the Percheron, there was a cross old gray horse next door to him, who looked down his nose at Joey because Joey knew so little about farm life.

One day, when he wasn't pulling a plow, because it was Sunday, Joey saw several people picnicking in the meadow. He decided to join them, for they looked as if they came from the City, and he thought they might have a lump of sugar in one of their pockets.

When he reached the spot they had gone for a walk, so he ate up their lunch.

When they came back, they were very angry and Joey was shut up in his stall for the rest of the day. He didn't even have a window to look out of.

He was lonely for his friends, the Policeman, and the ladies who patted him on the nose.

"I don't think I belong in the country after all,"

He was lonely for the high-bred horses, and all the interesting sights of the City.

sighed Joey. "I am now more discontented than ever."

Next day he heard the honk of a horn. He looked from the door of the barn, and whom should he see but Mr. Polaski, getting out of the truck!

"I have come for Joey," Mr. Polaski told the farmer. "I cannot get any more tires for my truck, so I think I will sell fruit and vegetables from my wagon again."

My goodness, but Joey was happy!

He went back to the City with Mr. Polaski and got into the elevator and up he went to the fourth floor of the big brick building. There was his stall, and there was the window for him to look out of.

And there was
the friendly Percheron.

"Welcome back, Joey,"
exclaimed the Percheron.
"I have missed you.

The Policeman has missed you.

The lady customers have missed you,

and so have
the children
in the playgrounds
and the parks."

"Tell me, how did you like the country?"

"The country is all right for country animals,"
Joey said,
"but I guess I am just a City horse at heart."

And he was never discontented again.

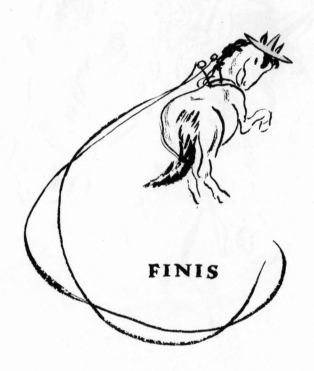

FINIS